Wicked Chic

Vivian French was best known at school for talking too much. She continued her attachment to words by becoming first an actor, then a story-teller and finally a writer of children's books . . . she's not sure how many she's written, but it's more than a hundred. She now travels all over the world telling stories and swapping ideas about books and writing with children and adults. And she still talks too much.

*Shock Shop is a superb collection of short,
illustrated, scary books for most younger readers by some
of today's most acclaimed writers for children.*

Other titles in Shock Shop:

Stealaway K. M. Peyton
The Bodigulpa Jenny Nimmo
Long Lost Jan Mark
You Have Ghost Mail Terence Blacker
The Beast of Crowsfoot Cottage Jeanne Willis
Goodbye, Tommy Blue Adèle Geras

Look out for

The Ghost of Uncle Arvie Sharon Creech
Olly Spellmaker and the Hairy Horror Susan Price
Olly Spellmaker and the Sulky Smudge Susan Price
Phantom Fun! Jon Burchett & Sara Vogler
Watch Out! Dina Anastasio & Jane O'Connor

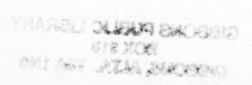

Wicked Chickens

Vivian French

Illustrated by John Bradley

MACMILLAN CHILDREN'S BOOKS

For Polly, the perfect editor – with love and clucks

First published 2003 by Macmillan Children's Books

This edition published 2003 by Macmillan Children's Books
a division of Macmillan Publishers Limited
20 New Wharf Road, London N1 9RR
Basingstoke and Oxford
www.panmacmillan.com

Associated companies throughout the world

ISBN 0 330 41575 1

5 7 9 8 6 4

A CIP catalogue record for this book is available from
the British Library.

Typeset by Intype Libra Ltd
Printed and bound in Great Britain by Mackays of Chatham plc, Kent

Contents

Chapter 1
Watch out! Dreams can come true

Would you believe it?

My Dad won at bingo. What's more, he won first prize. He won money. BIG money.

My sisters – I've got five – were over the moon. Dad marched in through the door with this silly smile on his face and a white envelope in his hand, and said "I've WON!!!" They nearly squashed him to death on the spot, they hugged him so hard. Then they rushed around in little circles asking if we were going to live in a house with a swimming pool, and if we were going to have our own aeroplane, and when could they have new TVs and stuff like that.

I said, "So what are we going to get first?"

Dad gave a huge, happy sigh, smiled the sort of smile you could use to light the London Christmas lights, and said, "I'm going to make my dream come true."

It was then I noticed Mum was looking a bit grim. She didn't look at all like someone who was going to share in a massive cash prize. It was really odd. She kept looking at Gran's tatty old teapot cosy on the top of the cupboard. I had a quick squint myself, but it was just the same old cosy – a horrible knitted thing meant to look like a thatched cottage with roses at the door and chickens scratching about outside. And exactly at the moment I was looking, Dad got up from his chair – still beaming – and guess what? He walked straight over to the cupboard and picked up the cosy. He stroked it as if it was his favourite pet, and then he plonked it right in the middle of the table.

"Take a look at *that*," he said. "*That's* what

I'm spending the money on. *That's* where we're going to live from now on. Happy ever after."

We all stared at him. Well, all of us kids. Mum went on looking grim. At last Ally said, "We're going to live in a *tea cosy?*"

Dad threw back his head and laughed and laughed. "Do you hear that, Marion?" he chortled at Mum. "Live in a tea cosy! Did you ever hear the like? Well I never!" He did some more ho-ho-ho-ho-ing.

Mum folded her arms and glared at him.

"You'd better tell them," she said. "If you really mean what you say, that is." For a second she looked hopeful. "It's OK to change your mind, you know."

"Change my mind?" Dad was glaring at Mum now. "Me? *Never*! I've been dreaming of living in a cottage like this for forty years, and now at last my dream's come true." He winked at us kids, and went back into super-smiley mode. "Ever since my mother – your nan, that is – bought this tea cosy, I've dreamed of living in a house exactly like it. Roses at the door, chickens scratching about in the dust outside." He breathed an ecstatic sigh. "And now it's all going to come true and we'll all live happily ever after, just like in the books."

There was a long pause. Then Laura said, "We're not going to move to the *country*, are we?" She made it sound like a snake-infested swamp.

Dad's smile faded a little. "You don't find

4

pretty little places like this in the middle of Tilney High Street, you know."

"But we *can't* live in the country!" Susie was turning a fiery pink. "How will we get to school? How will I see my friends?"

"There are other schools," Dad said. "You'll make new friends. And I expect country schools will be much better too – more grass to run about on . . . er . . . not so many kids . . ." He looked at Mum for help, but she wasn't playing.

"DAD!" Susie was almost purple. "I'm *fourteen*! Since *when* did I run about on *grass*? That's the *stupidest* thing I've ever heard of!"

Dad's smile was definitely on the way out. He tried a second-rate grin at Tiff and Molly and Ally and me. "You can't wait, can you, my lovelies? All that fresh air! Cows in the fields . . ."

Molly frowned. "Will we have a swimming pool?"

"And a new TV each?" said Tiff. "A *big* one!"

"I want my own bedroom!" said Ally.

I thought it was time I had a say in the matter. "And a dog. You promised we'd get a dog if we ever moved out of town—"

"Hang on, hang on!" Dad was getting blustery. "Just a minute! Just listen to your old man, will you?" He picked up the tea cosy and waved it at us. "Cottages like this don't come cheap, you know. And . . . erm . . . it isn't like winning the lottery, either. It's going to take most of the cash to set us up in our dream home, but once we're there I just *know* it'll be the best thing for all of us."

And then, just as we were all coming up to the boil to say *he* might know that but *we* didn't, he silenced the lot of us. He flumped into his chair, and tears began to trickle down his face. He clutched that tatty old tea cosy to his chest and said with a little hiccup in his voice, "Oh, Marion, love – oh, kids . . . I'm *so* happy."

Well, that was it, wasn't it? How could we fight him after that? Even Mum tried to smile and be cheerful for the rest of the evening – which was just as well, because things started going wrong the very next day . . .

Chapter 2

When dreams aren't quite as dreamy as you'd hoped . . .

The first thing to go wrong was Dad's discovery that although he'd won what he thought was a HUGE amount of dosh, it wasn't enough to buy any kind of dream cottage. Not nearly enough. Dream cottages, it seems, are only for millionaires . . . at least, dream cottages with enough room for eight people. Dad huffed and puffed and rang up every estate agent in the telephone book, but it was always the same. No thatched cottages, even without the roses at the door.

"We could get a nice little terrace house here in Tilney," Mum said with a wistful expression on her face. "It would be my

8

dream come true to stop living in a top flat where the lifts don't work. Maybe a little terraced house somewhere near the shops . . ."

Dad shook his head and suddenly began to look like Ally does when someone asks her to eat Brussels sprouts. "If we can't find a cottage to buy then we'll rent one," he said. "I'll find us a cottage if it's the last thing I do." And three days later he did.

And five days later there we were, stuffed into Uncle Gareth's old van, suitcases and boxes of food piled in the back, driving to our new home.

You might expect to hear that we were all singing jolly songs and counting the miles until we got there – but we weren't. Mum was hanging on to her bag as if it was a lifebelt, and every so often she'd pull out various bits of paper covered with lists and telephone numbers and stare at them in a desperate kind of way. Laura was muttering

9

darkly into her mobile phone. Susie was having a row with Tiff because Tiff said Susie was taking up too much room and Molly was complaining loudly because Ally's tin box of story tapes was digging into her leg. Ally was listening to her Walkman with her eyes tightly shut. Dad was sitting in the front with a large map on his knees, saying things like, "I'm sure it would've been quicker if we'd taken the A659," and Uncle Gareth was saying things like, "If you want me to take a right-hand turn then don't tell me to turn left." I was sitting in the darkest part of the van, clutching a plastic bag and trying hard not to be sick as Uncle G swerved round corner after corner.

We seemed to be in the van for hours and hours. I don't know if it really was a long way to the cottage or if Dad and Uncle G just got lost a lot, but by the time we stopped it was beginning to get dark. We'd had one

quick break
for sandwiches
and a speedy pee
but we were all well
fed up with travelling
when Uncle G pulled on the
brakes with a final squeal. Dad
said – and his voice was trembling with
excitement – "Looks like this is it, folks!"

I have to admit that I was excited as Dad
opened the van doors. I mean, it was a kind
of adventure after all . . . and I think the

others felt the same. We bundled out of the van as fast as we could and Mum was in a hurry too. We staggered on to the road – our legs were all pins and needley from not being able to move for so long – and we looked around for Dad's dream cottage . . .

There it was.

It really was a dream. It was truly pretty – even I could see that. There was a fairy-tale twisty path between clumps of long, floaty grass, big pink roses tumbling all round the door and a thick, yellow thatched roof.

Twinkly, shiny windows had spotless curtains flapping in the breeze, and the bright blue front door was open wide. Inside we could see a fire blazing in a grate and the cosiest sitting room you could imagine.

"*Wow*," breathed Susie. "It's just like a picture book!"

Ally didn't wait. She heaved her tin box under her arm and rushed through the neat little gate and up the twisty path.

"First in!" she yelled, and we all dashed after her – just in time to bump *smack*! into her zooming back towards us, with a furious looking woman chasing behind her. *Crash*! went Ally's tin box and we all fell higgledy-piggledy over each other. It was a miracle that Mum and Dad didn't fall over too.

"What do you think you're *doing*?" shrieked the woman. "This is *private*! Go *away*!" Only she had such a posh voice that it sounded as if she was saying "Prayvit," and Susie and Tiff began to giggle.

Dad was so open-mouthed he couldn't say anything. It was Mum who had to step forward and try to sort things out.

"Excuse me," she said, "but isn't this Cluck Cottage?"

The woman stopped trying to shoosh Ally off the path, where she was desperately scooping up her scattered tapes. "Certainly *not*," she snapped. "This is Cluck *House*. The

cottage is behind here – you have to go *outside* our garden, along to the left and down the track."

"Ooops," Laura said, and Mum began apologizing. The woman didn't stay to listen. She stomped off back to the picture-book cottage and slammed the door behind her.

"Friendly neighbours you got," said Uncle Gareth, and he went on unloading our stuff from the van.

Dad was still desperately cheerful. "Doesn't matter," he said as he picked up a bulging case in each hand, "we don't need to talk to her.

We'll just do our own thing in our own place." And he marched along to the left, looking for the track. We went with him, and we saw our new home for the first time.

"Oh," said Dad.

"Oh *no*," said Mum.

"You're joking!" said Laura.

"It's falling down!" said Susie.

"This *can't* be right," said Tiff.

"*Yuck*!" said Molly.

"It's *horrible*!" said Ally.

And it was.

Have you ever seen those before-and-after pictures they do for advertisements?

Well, that's what Cluck Cottage was like. But only the "Before" picture. No path, just mud. No clumps of wispy grass, just heaps of bricks and rubble. No roses round the door, just cracks. No neat, yellow thatched roof, just greeny-grey soggy straw. And the windows were so thick with dust and grime you couldn't even see if there were any curtains.

"Strike me pink with a beanpole," said Uncle Gareth from behind us. "Did you *know* it was like this, Pete?"

Dad shook his head.

"He found in the paper," Mum said through gritted teeth. "'Fully furnished cottage for eight. Needs a little care and attention' – and he went and signed on the dotted line." She turned to Dad. "You got the key?"

Dad nodded, still speechless. He pulled the key out of his pocket and forced it into the lock. It turned with a horrible grating noise and the front door creaked open.

16

"Better see what's inside," Mum said and we followed her into the gloom.

The door opened straight into the kitchen. We stood in a row . . . and stared.

The good thing about it was that it was a big room and there was a big table in the middle with eight chairs round it. The bad things? Everything else. The ceiling was the colour of used tea bags and there were

17

hundreds of strange, twisted, dusty plants hanging from bent nails on the massive, black beams. The walls were covered in disgusting spotty purple paper that was peeling off like dead skin. Underneath we could see greyish white flaking plaster, like crumbling bone. The sink was stained dark brown and was cracked all over and one old crooked tap dripped rusty water into a pile of saucepans full of green mould. There wasn't a cooker – only a heap of rusty black metal in a corner.

Dad took a deep breath. "That's a nice-looking range," he said. "With a bit of a clean it'd be great. Warm up the whole place in no time, I shouldn't wonder."

Mum said nothing at all. She stood very, very still. Her mouth was so tightly shut it looked like a thin little line.

Ally burst into tears. "I want to go HOOOOOOOME," she wailed.

"Me too," said Molly.

"Yes," Laura said. "I'll tell Uncle G—"

Thud! Mum threw her handbag on the floor. We all jumped a mile – Mum *never* does things like that.

"You didn't tell them, did you, Pete?" she said, and her voice was shaking with anger. "Your father couldn't afford to buy the place outright so we're part-buying, part-renting it. This *is* our home."

There was a ghastly pause while we looked round again – and at exactly that moment Uncle G put his head round the door.

"Oi! Pete!" he said. "There's six chickens out in the back garden!"

A strange expression floated over Dad's face – half guilt, half thrilled excitement. "Yes," he said, "I know."

Mum gave a half-strangled shriek. "*Chickens*?"

Dad looked even guiltier. "They come with the cottage," he said. "Six chickens. That's how I *knew* this was our dream home!"

Chapter 3
Cluck cluck cluck

The row went on for ages. Mum told Dad he was irresponsible and useless, and what's more, how *could* he have lost all sense the minute he saw there'd be chickens. Dad yelled back that it was *his* money and *his* dream and it wouldn't be the same without the chickens. Then Laura and Susie and Tiff and Molly joined in, shrieking about school and friends and swimming pools and TVs, and Ally burst into tears all over again. Uncle G stayed for a moment and then shrugged and disappeared. I think I was the only one who heard the roar of the van engine as he abandoned us to our fate.

I thought about Tilney and our wonderful,

 20

homely, comfortable, cosy flat as the sound of the van faded away behind the noise of my family shouting at each other. A cold, clammy hand clutched at my stomach. Laura, Susie, Tiff and Molly were always moaning and I was used to that – it seems to be something that happens as soon as you get to secondary school – but now Dad and Mum were fighting as well and my little sister Ally was still howling her eyes out.

I decided to go outside to look at the chickens.

Standing in a circle in the back garden were four scrawny looking brown birds, a speckly one and one that was black and white. I'd never seen chickens close up before, so I had a good squint at them . . . and do you know what? I wasn't sure I liked them very much. They had beady eyes with yellow rims and long, yellow, scaly legs with sharp claws. Their beaks were curved and shiny and there were odd, red, rubbery flaps on the top of their heads. They didn't look at all like the fluffy, fat hens on Gran's tea cosy.

The six of them swivelled their heads and stared hard at me, first with one sharp eye, and then the other.

Then the biggest brown chicken winked at me.

I'm not making it up, I promise. That chicken winked, and it wasn't the kind of jolly wink that Uncle G does – a "Hello, aren't we going to have fun together?" sort of wink. It

looked horribly like "You don't know anything about anything, kid – but *we* do."

I moved away.

There was a loud sniffing and Ally came stumping up.

"Ooo," she said. "Aren't they sweet?"

"They're disgusting," said Tiff. She and Molly were standing on the edge of the mud and they weren't looking too impressed.

"They've got horrible feet," Molly said. "Look at those claws!"

"What's Dad want a whole lot of chickens for, anyway?" Tiff asked.

"It's his dream," I said. "You know – chickens clucking round the door."

Molly made a face. "Huh! He'd have been better off getting a whole load of decorators and house cleaners in," she said. "Does he really expect us to sleep in this dump?"

"AAAAAAAAAAAAAAAAAAAAAAAAGH!"

The scream echoed across the garden. The

chickens fluttered wildly and Tiff and Molly clutched each other.

An upstairs window in the cottage was flung open, and Laura's face appeared. She was white as a sheet and screeching like a banshee. We could see Susie behind her and she was yelling too. Ally and I dashed inside to see what was going on. Mum and Dad were already halfway up the rickety wooden stairs and we flew up behind them. We found Laura and Susie in the room at the top. They were both balanced on a very small chair near the window, and they sounded like a couple of police sirens trying to outdo each other.

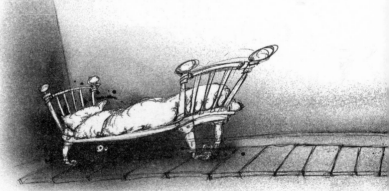

"WHAT is it?" asked Dad.

Susie stopped screaming and began to cry – her loudest, wailiest sort of crying. "It's . . . it's a MOUSE!"

"A HUGE one!" Laura moaned. "It was probably a rat, it was so big! And it's under that bed over there and I want to go home *now*!"

I waited for Mum to make the soothing noises she always makes when the girls meet spiders, or slugs, or beetles, or – although they hadn't ever met them before – mice. Strangely, though, she didn't. She looked at

Laura and Susie wobbling on the chair and she said, "Do you know what? I think we're all going to have to get busy. If we're going to live here we've got to pull together and get this place into some kind of order. I suggest you two begin by seeing if you can find some firewood while I have a look at that stove." She turned to Dad. "And *you'd* better help them before it gets pitch-black out there."

Nobody said anything. It just wasn't like Mum to sound fierce. Bossy. In charge.

Dad gave a little cough. He sounded as if he wasn't sure what to say. "Erm . . . yes, love. I'll sort it out, and then I'll have a look at that range." He coughed again. "I'm sure it'll be fine if we all try our best . . ." His voice died away as he trotted off down the stairs.

Mum looked at Laura and Susie. "Well?" she said.

Laura got off the chair first. She wasn't looking happy and as soon as she reached floor level safely she stuck out her chin.

"Do you know what?" she said. "I never wanted to come here, and I think you're mean, mean, *mean* to make us stay. Susie and I *hate it* and we want to go home and if we can't go home we want to stay in a hotel. Dad's got money, hasn't he? Tell him we want to be comfortable, not to live in a gross, disgusting slum!"

Susie nodded, and jumped down beside Laura. "It's not fair, Mum – you have to tell Dad! Why should he wreck everyone's life? We didn't want to live in a tea-cosy cottage – he never even asked us!" And she grabbed Laura's hand and they sat down together with a *flump*! on one of the beds. A cloud of dust flew up into the air and we all began to cough as if we had some kind of bubonic plague.

Mum recovered first and the dust seemed to have knocked some of the fight out of her. "I know it's awful," she said, "but we're stuck here for the moment."

"Why are we?" Tiff's head appeared at the

top of the stairs, with Molly just behind her. "Mum, have you *seen* the sitting room? The wallpaper's peeling off there as well, and there isn't even a TV!"

"That's right," Molly said. "It's totally revolting. We've *got* to go somewhere else."

"I'm going to tell Dad," Laura said. "I'm going to make him listen!" And she strode across the floor towards the stairs.

Mum slumped against the wall. "It's no good," she said. "We haven't got any transport, and even if we had we can't go and stay in a hotel. Dad's used most of his winnings to pay for this place." She sighed such an enormous sigh it was almost enough to clear the dust away.

"We *can't* stay in this place!" Laura's voice reached screech level. "Do you know you can't even get a mobile phone signal here? I'm going to *tell* him! Come on, you lot, you come too!" She marched towards the stairs, Susie close behind her, with Tiff and Molly falling

 28

into rank as she got to the bottom.

Mum sighed another huge sigh. "It won't do any good," she said. "Your dad's been dreaming of a cottage for so long he really and truly can't see what this one's like. We'll just have to make the best of it, and maybe he'll change his mind eventually." She hauled herself upright. "I'd better go and see if I can get that kitchen clean."

I didn't know if she was talking to me, or to herself. It's often like that with Mum. Because me and Ally are younger than the others she goes on talking to us after they've stormed off somewhere. It's a bit like we mop up what's left over in her thoughts.

"Maybe we can help him change his mind?" I suggested, but Mum was already halfway down the stairs. Ally lay down on her front and peered into the dust under one of the beds.

"I'm going to catch the mouse and train him to do tricks," she said, and giggled. "Maybe I can train him to sit on Laura's pillow!"

29

I left her to it and went downstairs to have another look at the chickens.

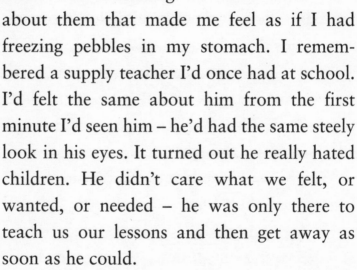

It was odd. I couldn't get them out of my mind. There was something about them that made me feel as if I had freezing pebbles in my stomach. I remembered a supply teacher I'd once had at school. I'd felt the same about him from the first minute I'd seen him – he'd had the same steely look in his eyes. It turned out he really hated children. He didn't care what we felt, or wanted, or needed – he was only there to teach us our lessons and then get away as soon as he could.

I shook my head. Stupid to think about that – chickens were only birds, after all. Egg-laying machines. And they were part of Dad's dream, so surely they couldn't be altogether bad.

As I came out of the back door I saw my four big sisters push their way through the front gate and stomp off along the lane. It was too dark to see their faces but they were talking loudly about things being NOT FAIR. Molly had her fists clenched and Tiff was waving her arms. It was pretty clear their chat with Dad hadn't gone the way they'd hoped.

Chapter 4
From bad to worse

Dad was outside sorting out bits of wood and the chickens were watching him with their heads on one side. Every so often one of them would peck at a plank and it sounded like a sharp little hammer. RAT A TAT TAT! RAT A TAT TAT!

As I came closer they shifted round and peered at me, doing that first-one-eye-and-then-the-other thing. They stared and stared without blinking and I stared back . . . but it was me who looked away first.

"Have you come to complain too?" Dad asked. He sounded fed up.

"Not really. Want a hand?"

Dad grunted. "See if you can find anything

32

useful in that shed over there. I need some sort of fencing to make a chicken run." He straightened up and rubbed his nose, leaving a grubby smear. "Of course, once your mother gets used to them being here, they can run free. They're used to that, after all." The dream-coming-true smile floated back on to his face. "Just think, Charlie – freshly laid eggs for breakfast."

I nodded, and tracked my way through the mud and weeds to the end of the garden. The shed was quite large and when I finally got the outside bolts to shift and the door to open I was surprised to find it wasn't too bad inside – there was even a light switch. I turned it on and I could see dusty tools hung on hooks, and a table, and two quite comfy looking chairs. It looked as if the last people to live in the cottage had used the shed as an escape – and I could quite see why. I nearly called Dad and suggested we move into the shed too . . . but something told me he wouldn't think it was funny.

There wasn't any fencing but there was a rusty looking bundle of wire netting behind an old wooden ladder. I lugged the bundle out and Dad went even dreamier.

"Just the thing," he said, "that's perfect. See, Charlie? Everything we could possibly need!" And it was surprising how quickly Dad arranged the netting into a square and nailed it to some posts he'd already bashed into place.

"There." He looked towards the chickens. "Come on, girls. Time to see your new home!" He stopped for a moment. "Tell you what, Charlie, why don't you get them in?"

I put out my hand to attract them, as you would a dog or cat. I didn't know what else to do. I didn't really want to have to round them up, but I knew Dad thought he was giving me a special treat and I didn't want to hurt his feelings. The chickens backed away, staring again, and their eyes glittered in the semi-darkness. I swallowed hard.

Not one chicken came into the muddy run. Dad made little encouraging clucking noises but they took no notice. They clustered in a huddle and made strange little tutting noises at each other.

"Maybe they're talking about us," I said, and part of me was sure they were.

Dad laughed. "That's right. They're saying how brilliant it is to live in a dream cottage!"

That wasn't quite what I'd thought but I didn't say anything.

"Well, I'll leave you to it," Dad went on, "and I'll go and give Mum a hand with the range." He looked up at the cottage. "Or maybe I should have a look at that roof first. Seems to me there are one or two patches that might spring a leak if it rains tonight. Was there a ladder in the shed?"

"Yes," I said. It would have been a lot better if there'd been a whole new roof there too. Dad pottered happily off, whistling under his breath.

"Charlie!" Mum was yelling from the house.

"Charlie, can you see any wood out there? Or coal? Or anything that might burn?"

I left the chickens and began hunting around. There were quite a lot of old sticks and logs stacked against the back wall, so I grabbed as many as I could and took them in to Mum. She was standing over the heap of metal that Dad had called "the range", and she was covered in dust and smuts but she'd done wonders. The range was looking like the kind of ancient cooker you see in history books instead of a pile of junk.

"Thanks, Charlie," Mum said, and sighed heavily. "Let's see if we can get this to work."

Ten minutes later there was a little glow of warmth and Mum was just a teeny bit more cheerful. If you stood about ten centimetres away from the flames you could even feel quite hot . . . but I didn't see how it was going to heat

the whole house. Still, it was better than nothing. Mum grinned at me, and gave me a thumbs up as she marched towards the horrible sink.

"Maybe we'll get this place sorted after all," she said. At that very moment there was a scraping slithery noise, and we saw a ladder slide past the back window with Dad hanging on to it.

Mum said a word that I'd never heard her use before, and shot out of the kitchen. I zoomed after her. We found Dad flat on his back on the ground and the ladder lying on top of him.

"OW! OW! OW!" Dad moaned. Mum heaved the ladder away.

"What on *earth* do you think you were doing?" she snapped. "It's *dark*! It'd serve you right if you were *dead*!"

Dad got slowly to his feet. "My back," he groaned. "It really hurts, Marion."

Mum folded her arms and looked about as sympathetic as the cottage wall. "How stupid can you be, Pete Smithers?" she asked. "Almost pitch-dark and you go climbing up a *ladder*? Haven't we got enough to do without you doing your best to kill yourself?"

"I was trying to look at the roof," Dad said. "I'm sorry . . . I'm going to have to sit down." He staggered into the kitchen, and collapsed on to one of the chairs. "Charlie, love – how are the chickens?"

I realized I didn't know if they'd gone into their run or not. I gave a quick glance out of the window. The chickens were standing in a row behind the wire netting – and they were laughing.

I'm not exaggerating. They were laughing. There was no doubt about it. They were flapping their scrappy wings and throwing their heads back with their beaks wide open and

38

cackling loud harsh cackles. They were laughing their heads off.

"Um . . ." I said. The cold hand was back inside my stomach. "Dad," I said, "are chickens always like that? They're . . . they're making a very odd noise."

Dad put his hand to his ear and listened. He smiled happily. "They're just pleased to have a proper run," he said, and he looked like a small kid about to be given chocolate buttons. "Hey! Maybe they've laid an egg! Quick, go and have a look – they make loads of noise when they've laid an egg."

Mum snorted. "They won't have laid anything yet," she said. "They're much too young! As chickens go, those are still teenagers! And what do you know about keeping hens, anyway? You've never even had a budgerigar!"

"I've been reading up on it," Dad told her huffily. He put his hand on my arm and lowered his voice. "Just pop out and have a look, Charlie." He rolled his eyes. "Your poor old dad's in agony here."

"And whose fault is that?" Mum was as icy as the North Pole. "And what's more, who's going to look after those birds if you're in here with a bad back?"

"Hang on a moment! It was an *accident*!" Dad retorted. "And those birds are fine! They've been looking after themselves ever since the last people left, haven't they?" He sounded so angry I thought I'd slide away . . .

And as I tiptoed towards the staircase up to the bedrooms, the rowing broke out all over again. Only worse. You could hear every

single word floating up through the floorboards into the rooms above.

As I crept into the first bedroom, I saw Ally retreating under a dusty blanket with her Walkman firmly clamped over her ears and her thumb in her mouth. I made a sympathetic face at her and decided to distract myself by exploring.

Each room had one single electric bulb swinging from a wire. Shadows followed me round as I opened doors and tiptoed across creaky wooden floors. Twice I nearly went back to persuade Ally to come with me. There was a funny little staircase like a built-in stepladder that went up into the roof, but although there were four tiny rooms up there, they were quite empty. On the floor below – where Ally was hiding out – there were only two bedrooms, with four beds in each one – which didn't seem to me to be the most ideal way of living. The idea of sharing with Mum and Dad and Ally wasn't a thrill. The idea of sharing with Laura or Susie or Molly or Tiff gave me the shivers.

The yelling was still going on downstairs so I tried what I'd thought was a cupboard door and found a bathroom, with the most ancient bath I'd ever seen in my entire life. Mum and Dad's voices were more muffled in there, so I collected two pillows and settled myself in the bath with a book from my backpack. It wasn't very warm but at least it was comfortable and peaceful – that is, until Laura and the others came back.

That was when World War Three broke out. However hard I tried to concentrate on my story I couldn't help but hear that we were living in the Dark Ages and there were no shops for a thousand miles and nothing to look at except sheep and chickens and cows and it was HORRIBLE and AWFUL and GROSS and DISGUSTING.

The shouting got louder. It turned out the girls had found a local garage and bought sweets. Mum pounced and wanted to know if the garage sold things like bleach and scrubbing brushes and disinfectant. Tiff and Molly said they hadn't noticed because they were so unhappy.

"We didn't notice either," Laura said. "Why should we?"

"No," said Susie. "We're not interested in stuff like cleaning things. We're not slaves."

AAAAAAAAAGH!

The windows shook in their frames, dust rose in clouds and the whole house creaked as

Mum let everyone know *who* was being treated like a slave, and *exactly* what she felt about it. It was round about then that Ally came to join me in the bath. And two minutes after that there was a manic knocking on the front door.

Chapter 5
Four and two make more than six

Ally and I looked at each other and we fairly leaped out of the bath. Whoever it was had finally stopped the riot downstairs. I don't know about Ally, but I wanted to hug them, and if I'm completely truthful I had a tiny flickering hope that it might be Uncle Gareth come back to collect us and take us home.

I changed my mind big time about the hugging when Mum opened the door and I saw who was there. It was the woman from Cluck House and with her was a big bloke in a smart blue blazer with twinkly gold buttons.

"I say," the bloke said. "You can't go on making a row like that, you know. We're here on our hols, and it's a ter'ble bore having all that noise. We've had ten days' peace and quiet, don'tcha know, and we don't want our last days ruined."

The woman pushed in front of him. "*And* you've got chickens! I hope you know live animals are *not* allowed? Besides, there are *far* too many in that ridiculous little run! It's positively cruel. But then . . ." she smirked at Mum, "I don't suppose you town people know about things like that."

Mum took a deep breath. "My husband and I are in the process of buying this cottage," she said, and her voice was pure acid. "I'm sorry if my children are noisy, but there's a great deal to be done here. The cottage wasn't at all in the condition we expected. As for the chickens, they were here when we arrived. They came with the cottage. My husband has every intention of providing them with a proper hen house tomorrow. Now, I think that's everything dealt with, so I'll wish you good evening." And Mum slammed the door in their faces.

"*Wow!*" I said admiringly.

"Hurrah for Mum!" Ally cheered.

"What does she mean, 'too many

chickens'?" Dad wanted to know. "What does she expect? A blooming palace for every little feathered friend?"

Mum picked up a broom with half its bristles missing and began sweeping the floor as if she was swishing our neighbours away down the path. "Never mind them," she said. You could still have sliced a pineapple with her voice, it was so sharp. "I don't *ever* want to be shown up like that again – do you all understand? Susie! Laura!" She pointed the brush at the girls, who were whispering to each other. "You can start on the washing up. Scrub those saucepans and Tiff and Molly can go upstairs and start sorting out the beds. We'll have an early night and start cleaning this place properly from top to bottom tomorrow morning. And that means *all* of us."

Susie and Laura began rattling saucepans in the sink with surprising enthusiasm. They scrubbed and rubbed and then Laura dug

48

Susie in the ribs with her elbow.

Uh uh, I thought. Something's up.

"Did you hear what that man said, Mum?" Susie asked, and her very best Mum-pleasing smile spread from ear to ear. "He said they're on their holidays, so that must mean that's a holiday cottage – they don't live there all the time!"

"Yes!" Laura was just as smiley. "So when they move out—"

"WE CAN MOVE IN!" they said together, and they clashed a couple of pans for emphasis.

"Is that true?" Ally pulled at Mum's arm. "Can we go and live in the fairy-tale cottage?"

"That'd be all right." Tiff stopped hauling suitcases across the floor. "I don't mind living there. Well, not nearly so much."

"They've got a dishwasher," Molly said as if she was talking about the crock of gold at the end of the rainbow. "I saw it through the doorway when we thought it was our house."

There was a pause, except for Mum's fearsome sweeping. She didn't say a word. Dad gave one of his awkward coughs.

"Sorry, kids." He shook his head. "That place is booked all summer. This one – our one – was the only thatched cottage that was empty." He noticed the freezing chill from his four oldest daughters. "Don't look like that, girls. This place'll be fabulous with a lick of paint. Tell you what, tomorrow you can decide what colour you want your bedroom!"

That started the arguing all over again, except that this time even Ally joined in. Mum looked so ferocious they didn't shout and yell, but the hissed whispering was worse. It was like snakes fighting.

I thought about going back to my bath but I'd have had to climb over the pile of suitcases Tiff and Molly had dumped at the foot of the stairs. It seemed easier to go outside. It was dark out there now but there was enough light from the kitchen window to see that the chickens were out in their run.

I stopped.

I stared.

I gawped.

I gaped.

The run was *full* of chickens. And they were all squawking and cackling and flapping and strutting about. They looked – I could only think of one word – triumphant.

I took a deep breath, took a step nearer, and rubbed my eyes. Was I seeing things? No. There had been

six chickens before . . . now there were ten. I could see the speckly one and the black-and-white one – and eight brown ones, all alike. I could no more have said which were here first than I could have grown wings myself. As I got nearer they grew suddenly silent. They froze into complete stillness and all ten watched me to see what I was going to do next . . . watched me with those strange glittering eyes.

I shook my head. My heart was doing odd little jumps in my chest and I desperately wanted to believe I'd made some kind of mistake. Maybe the extra chickens had been hiding?

Yes! That must be it! After all, I could easily have missed seeing them – couldn't I?

I turned round and went straight back into the house. It might be damp and dreary and dusty and full of my arguing sisters but at least there was electric light throwing a friendly yellow square into the darkness.

Inside it was quieter than I'd expected. Dad was still slumped in his chair but Mum was stirring something in a saucepan on the range and Ally was putting plates on the table. There was no sign of the others.

Ally grinned at me. "Beans on toast," she said. "You can do the toast."

I looked round for a toaster but of course there wasn't one. Ally's grin grew wider. "You've got to use that," she said, and she pointed to a bag of sliced bread and a bendy wire fork with a long handle.

I picked up the fork and speared a slice of bread.

"Dad," I said cautiously, "how many chickens did you say came with the cottage?"

Dad tried to sit up, and made a faint moaning noise. Mum glanced in his direction but didn't say anything. She just stirred the beans harder.

"Six," Dad said. "Doing all right, are they? Did you check for eggs?"

"No eggs," I said, "but there's something odd going on. There's ten of them now."

Dad's eyebrows whizzed up his forehead. "*Ten*? Ten chickens?"

"Yes," I said.

Dad looked puzzled. "Strange."

"Maybe their friends have flown in to see them," Ally suggested cheerfully.

Dad's face cleared. "It'll be something like that. Didn't Molly say something about seeing chickens when they were out on their walk?"

"Oh!" I suddenly felt much lighter all over. "Oh, *yes*. Yes, that must be it."

"You're burning the toast," Ally warned me, and I flipped the bread over and picked up another slice.

"This is OK," I said as I waved it in front of the steady glow of the flames. The kitchen still looked dreadfully bleak but I was feeling positively toasty myself. The smell of baked beans was beginning to fill the air and my tummy rumbled. "Have we got any grated cheese?"

"I'll do it," Ally said, and she skipped off to ferret about in one of the many cardboard boxes Mum had brought with us.

I looked at my growing pile of toast. "How many more pieces should I do?"

"Enough for just us," Mum said, and she sounded so strange that I got up to have a look at her. She gave me a tired smile. "Laura and the others are upstairs. They say they're on strike, so we'll just let them get on with it. I've had enough of all this stupid arguing." She wiped her hand across her forehead. "Beans on toast with grated cheese for four – coming up!"

Chapter 6

Things are always better in the morning . . . aren't they?

I yawned, stretched and opened my eyes . . .

Where was I?

The ceiling above me was cracked and grey and festooned with ancient spiders' webs. I yawned again, and stuck my head out from under the blankets. Ally was curled up, fast asleep, in a metal-framed bed next to mine. Across the room were two more of the same beds – a bit like hospital beds – and Dad was snoring steadily in one, while Mum was flat out in the other. I sat up cautiously and inspected my surroundings. Yes, I was in Dad's dream cottage but no one had kissed the frog yet and turned the "before" into the "after". The beds were hard and lumpy.

56

There hadn't been any sheets when we looked the night before. Mum had told us to shake out the blankets and hope for the best. I checked carefully. Good. No bites.

The toilet was downstairs and through the kitchen, so I threw on my clothes and headed for the stairs. Halfway down I heard the sound of whispering voices – I guessed that Laura and Co. were awake. I wondered what they were planning. They hadn't had anything to eat the night before, I thought, so they must be starving . . . but when I reached the kitchen I saw that they'd been looking after themselves OK. There was nothing left in the bread wrapper except the crust and the jam pot was empty too. Their dirty plates were heaped by the sink. Typical, I thought crossly. I'd been hoping for toast and jam for breakfast.

As I came back from the toilet to wash my hands in the kitchen sink I thought I heard rain.

"Odd," I said to myself. The sky had been bright blue outside my bedroom window, even

57

through a hundred years of grime. I looked at the front kitchen window to check. No, no rain . . . but the noise was louder. It didn't sound exactly like rain pattering on the ground but that was the only thing I could think of . . . or maybe it was more like a giant fluttering?

Fluttering . . . ?

My heart flew into my mouth, and my stomach clenched. I'd been pushing all thoughts of the chickens to the back of my mind. I'd convinced myself it was a sunny day, everything was fine, I must have imagined all the odd things that had happened the day before . . . the way you do. But now it was all rushing back, and I felt sick as I turned round to look out of the back window – the one that overlooked the garden.

Chickens.

They were on top of the shed, and the run was heaving. They were perched on the wire, and they were strutting about in the mud by the back door. Automatically I began to count

58

them. One, two, three . . . eighteen. Sixteen brown, one speckled, one black and white. Eighteen chickens, all flapping their wings at each other in a steady rhythm.

Flap, flap, flap-a-flap, flap. Flap, flap, flap-a-flap, flap.

I couldn't bear it. I headed up those stairs as if every single chicken was after me, pecking at my ankles.

"Mum! Dad!"

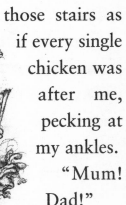

Mum came out in a hurry, her hair standing on end. "Charlie? What is it? Are you all right?"

"It's the chickens!" I gasped. "There's *more* of them!"

I could see Mum collapsing back into super-tired mode as she winched up a smile. "Oh,

Charlie, is that all? They've probably come in from a local farm." She rubbed at her arms. "Ouch. I'm aching all over. Go and see if the range is still alight, there's a poppet. And put the kettle on if it is. I'm dying for a cuppa." She turned round to stagger back to bed.

I stared after her as she disappeared. Was I in the middle of some dreadful nightmare that none of the rest of my family had anything to do with? Those chickens were not ordinary chickens. No way. So why was everyone else ignoring them, or talking about farms, or finding reasonable explanations? It didn't make sense.

Molly came out of the other bedroom and waved at me sleepily.

"Anyone in the loo?" she asked.

"No," I said.

"Good." She pushed past me but in quite a friendly way. She may be Tiff's twin but on her own she's about the best of the four of them. I made a snap decision and went down to the

kitchen behind her. I waited by the window until she'd come back out of the toilet.

"Moll," I said, "can I show you something a bit peculiar?"

"S'pose so," she said.

"Well – look out of the kitchen window. The back one."

Molly wandered over to the window, looked out and froze.

"What's happened to the chickens? There's hundreds of them!"

"I know," I said miserably.

"And why are they doing that flapping thing?" Molly was beginning to sound almost as freaked as I was. "That's WEIRD!"

"I tried to tell Mum, but she thinks it's OK."

"Well, it isn't." Molly zipped up her hood in grim determination. "I'll get Laura. We've had more of this place than we can stand and moronic weirdo chickens are the last straw. We're going back home, whatever Mum and Dad say." She looked aghast.

"Whoops! Shouldn't have told you that . . .
Laura'll kill me."

It was my turn to look horrified. "How can
you go home? What about Mum and Dad?"

Molly turned away from the window and
sighed. "Laura and Susie say we can hitch a
ride to the nearest station and then we've got
enough money for a train home. Hopefully."
She gave me a quick and surprising hug. "It's
not that we want to leave you, Charlie, but it's
not so bad for you – you and Ally are just kids.
We've got none of our friends here and there's
no shops and it's filthy dirty and *horrible*." Her
voice wobbled. "And Dad never even *asked* us
if we wanted to come!" She pulled away from
me and walked off, but I knew she was crying.

I didn't know what to say. All I could think
of was Dad's face when he talked about his
dream coming true . . . and how glowing he'd
been. At the same time I knew Molly was
right. Dad hadn't asked any of us.

*

"Charlie! QUICK!" Molly's voice was a high-pitched squeal. "Come and LOOK!" She was at the garden window and her eyes were like saucers. I rushed to see what she was looking at, although I knew it would be the chickens. It was.

Twelve of the brown chickens were in a circle, but the remaining four were in the middle, and they were behaving in the most peculiar way. They kept running towards each other, then – just as they were about to crash together – they'd stop, make a throaty squawk, and run backwards. Backwards for about ten steps, then *squawk*! run towards each other again. The ones on the outside were glaring at them and shifting from scaly claw to scaly claw. If one of the running chickens got too close to the chickens on the outside, they slashed down with their curvy beaks and pecked as hard as they could.

I found I was hanging on to Molly's hand. It was horrible, but we couldn't stop watching

63

. . . and then the weirdest thing of all happened. It was so weird that my brain gave a violent stagger and actually hurt.

All four brown chickens paused as near to the edge of the circle as they dared. Then they gave a mad, ear-splitting screech and ran towards each other faster than ever – but when they met they didn't stop.

POUF!

There was one chicken left.

Four chickens had turned into one. Then that one gave its feathers a good shake, cluck-clucked in a normal, everyday, chickenish sort of way and began scratching in the dust. The speckly chicken and the black-and-white one fluttered down to join it, but the others wheeled round as if they'd been given an order, and marched back to the run.

I tried to swallow, but my throat wouldn't work properly. Molly was white as a sheet.

"I think I'm dreaming," she said at last, and her voice was croaky. "That can't have happened. I know it can't."

I shook my head to clear it. "It is very early in the morning."

"Yes," Molly said. "Yes." She looked in silence at the three ordinary chickens pottering about in the weedy mud outside. "We must have imagined it."

"MOLL!" There was a yell from upstairs. Laura's voice. "Molly, have you died down there?"

Molly grabbed my arm with a sudden urgency. "Charlie! Promise you won't tell Mum and Dad what I told you?" she whispered. "*Promise?*"

"OK," I said, but I wasn't thinking about the girls' plans for escape as Molly zoomed off. Wild and extraordinary ideas were tumbling round and round inside my brain and I desperately needed space to sort them out.

65

Chapter 7
Getting rid of Mum and Dad

The thoughts I was having were so stupendously amazing that I had to sit down and hold my head. There was a severe danger of my brains being squeezed out of my ears. The way my thoughts were going was like this:

What if the multiplying chickens were something to do with my sisters?

At first it was too weird to take seriously, but the more I thought about it the more it seemed a possibility. The worse they got, the more chickens there were. But this morning when Molly had been positively human, four chickens had voomphed into one . . . one ordinary one.

And if it had happened once it could happen again.

Then there was my next thought.

There was something different about the speckly chicken and the black-and-white one.

What?

And the only answer I could come up with was that they were, in some fantastic way, connected with Ally and me. But which of us was which? And did it matter anyway?

Then I thought, what would happen if Laura and Susie and Tiff and Molly sneaked off back to Tilney?

Part of me saw horrible pictures of the whole countryside being full of millions of chickens and the other part thought, well – at least they'll be out of here. But then I pictured Dad and Mum and I knew deep down that it would be a really, really *terrible* thing if the girls did go. Dad's dream might be more of a nightmare at the moment, but if the girls ran home it wouldn't make anything any better. Dad had been dreaming of this cottage idea for – what had he said? – forty years. He

wasn't going to give up easily. If the girls went back to Tilney he'd only try and think of some other way of making his dream come true . . . and it could even be worse next time. What's more, he'd be even more pig-headed about it . . . and Mum would be even more miserable.

But how could I sort it all out?

And you may think it was big-headed of me that I thought I could – but who else was there?

There was a shuffling on the stairs, and Dad appeared in Mum's dressing gown. He looked awful. He was bent over like an old man, and he was grunting as if every step was agony.

"Got to have a pee," he muttered as he reached ground level. "My back's killing me. I'd sell my soul for an upstairs toilet."

I watched him stagger out and yet another shaft of brilliant inspiration hit me.

The shed!

If I could get Dad and Mum tucked away in

there, maybe I could start work on my sisters. But how? What if I got Dad out there first . . . there had to be a way . . .

A mad scramble into Mum's food boxes gave me an answer. I snatched up a massive bottle of oil and flung it on the concrete floor by the toilet door. It smashed into thousands of glassy splinters, and the oil spread out in a treacherous slidy lake.

Dad appeared through the door and I noticed his feet were bare. Good, I thought, and began to jabber excuses about the oil bottle slipping out of my hands when I was trying to start putting things away. Dad was in too much pain to ask questions. I couldn't help feeling sorry for him as he hung on to the door frame and stared in horror at the mess.

"Tell you what, Dad, I'll clear this up, I promise – but why don't you go and sit in one of the armchairs in the shed? They look dead comfortable, and it won't be far for you to come if you need another pee. And I'll bring you a cup of tea just as soon as the kettle's boiled . . ."

Dad must really have been feeling bad. He hardly said anything as I shoved his feet into a giant pair of old wellies I found by the door, and he leaned heavily on me all the way across the muddy garden. He didn't even look at his beloved chickens. That made me feel truly dreadful, as if I was doing something

 70

really sneaky. I did give them a quick side-ways glance as we passed the run but most of them were huddled together. When we got to the shed he sank into a chair with a massive sigh and managed a feeble smile.

"You're right," he said weakly. "This is comfortable. I'll just rest here until you've cleared up that mess." He closed his eyes.

"I'll be as quick as I can," I told him. I felt a bit better when he called after me, "Don't forget to check on the chickens. See if they've laid any eggs."

Having Dad already in the shed would make it easier to deal with Mum – at least, that's what I hoped. I hurried back across the garden. A low muttering was coming from the chicken run, but otherwise it seemed peaceful. I gave myself a thumbs up and headed for the kitchen.

I swept up the worst of the glass and oil with the tatty old broom and tipped the bits into the dustbin. I thought the floor looked much

better after I'd finished; it was quite shiny, rather as if it had been polished. I checked the range and stuffed some more twigs and bits of wood in. They flared up at once and I was surprised to find the flat cooking bit on the top was so hot that the water on the bottom of the kettle hissed and spat as I plonked it down.

But then, as I stood and waited for the kettle to boil, I began to wonder if I was mad. If Laura and Co. were determined to make their escape, how could I stop them? Whatever was I going to say? When had any of those four ever listened to me? And what about Mum? She almost always knew when I was up to something. It suddenly felt really scary and I wondered if I should give in and tell Mum what I knew . . . after all, aren't grown-ups meant to be able to sort things out? OK, my life wouldn't be worth living when Laura knew I'd sneaked on her and I couldn't even start to imagine what would happen to the chickens, but maybe I'd bitten off more than I could chew.

"Charlie? Is that tea made?"

Mum was coming down the stairs, dressed, and with her hair tied up on top of her head. She looked much more together, although she had dark shadows under her eyes.

"I'm just doing it," I said and poured the boiling water into the teapot. It was now or never. "Mum, about Laura and Susie and the twins . . ."

Mum snapped her fingers at me. "No telling tales," she said. "I'm sure they'll be OK today. They're all good girls, really – they won't want to let Dad down." She looked round, as if she was expecting to see Dad pop up from under the teapot. "Where *is* Dad, by the way? He's not still in the loo, is he?"

That was it. Mum didn't want me to tell tales. It was up to me to save my world.

I gave up worrying and just seized my opportunity.

"Dad's in the shed," I said. "Erm . . . he doesn't look very good, Mum. Maybe you

73

should see if he's OK."

"In the *shed*?" You can see why my sisters squeak when something exciting happens. Mum's voice was octaves above normal. "What's he doing in the shed?"

"Er . . . having a rest," I said truthfully. "Here's your tea. Why don't you take Dad a cup and you can see how he's doing?"

Mum made a noise something between a snort and a grunt, and took the other mug that I was holding out. I felt distinctly pleased with myself – until Mum's trainers hit the shiny oily patch on the floor. She saved herself by the skin of her teeth and a wild swerve, but tea and mugs splashed and crashed all over the place. I rushed to help her, and boy! was she angry. Luckily she decided that as Dad was the cause of all of our problems, she'd sort him out before she came back to deal with me. She stormed over the mud and I swear her feet didn't touch the ground. She whisked into the shed and I had to run like a greyhound to get to the door in time to slam it shut before she could reappear. As I pushed the bolts firmly home I could feel the storm clouds inside battering the wooden walls.

I looked anxiously at the chickens on my way back. They were definitely up to something. The speckly one and the black-and-white one were perched on the shed roof, but the others froze into stillness as I scuttled by. I didn't try to count them. I didn't want to know. There was something much too creepy about the way they didn't move a muscle until I was well past.

I leaped through the door and went down with a hideous THWACK! on to my backside.

There was a loud cackle and Susie and Tiff doubled up with laughter. Ally was buttering a biscuit and she did grin a bit, but then she hopped up to see if I was OK. For a couple of seconds I couldn't speak because there was no breath left in me. I sat up and gasped like a fish deprived of water.

"There's oil all over the floor," Ally told me. "It's very slidy." She went back to her biscuit. "Where're Mum and Dad?"

I took my first breath for what seemed like weeks. "In the shed."

"What's in there?" Susie asked. "More horrible chickens?"

If I hadn't been so winded by falling over I would never have told Susie and Tiff what I'd done. My brain was definitely unhinged at that moment.

"No," I said. "I've shut them in."

Three pairs of eyes stared at me in shock.

"You did WHAT?"

"I've shut Mum and Dad in the shed."

76

Chapter 8
Wicked chickens

Susie and Tiff went on staring for at least a minute, then grabbed each other.

"That's it!" said Susie.

"We can go NOW!" said Tiff, and she turned to Ally. "Ally, go and tell Laura and Molly to come down here quick – and say to bring the bags with them!"

Ally blew her biscuit crumbs off the table. "What bags?"

"Just do it!" Susie said. "RUN!"

Ally gave Susie a dirty look, but it's difficult to argue with someone of fourteen when you're only six. She did as she was told.

"What are you going to do?" I asked, although I already knew. The bottom of my stomach was cold and clammy and I was feeling sick. I'd made it *so* easy for them. How could I have been so *stupid*?

Susie was piling packets of biscuits into a plastic bag. "We're going back to Tilney," she said. "We're going to live at home with Uncle G and Auntie Cath until Dad sees sense. We're not staying here another second."

Laura and Molly came clumping down the stairs, Ally behind them.

"Thanks, Charlie," Laura said. "We were going to tell Mum we needed a walk – but this is *much* easier! Don't let her out for at least an hour, will you?"

I gulped. "Laura," I said, "I need to tell you about the chickens . . ." I hoped desperately that I sounded braver than I felt. "It's really important. Molly and I saw something ever so peculiar this morning—"

Laura wasn't listening. She ignored me completely, and swung her bag over her shoulder. "Everybody ready?" she asked.

"LAURA!" I was desperate. "*Please* listen to me, *please*! Or . . . or I'll go straight out and get Mum and Dad and tell them what you're up to!"

Laura sneered. "Oh no you won't," she said, "because if you do we'll just tell Mum you're lying. There're four of us – she'll never believe you. And then we'll make your life a total misery until you wish you'd never been born and in the end we'll find a way to go anyway, so it might as well be now."

I couldn't think of anything else to say. I sat where I was on the greasy floor, my stomach turning little somersaults inside me. I watched miserably as Laura, Susie, Tiff and Molly gathered the last of their bits together and headed for the front door.

Tiff waved, Molly blew me and Ally a kiss, and Laura pretended we didn't exist.

"Bye, kiddos," Susie said cheerfully. "Enjoy Doom Cottage!" She swung the front door open . . .

and SCREAMED.

So did Laura. And Molly. Tiff slammed the door shut and staggered back, her face a horrible greenish grey.

"Charlie!" Ally was clutching at my T-shirt and whispering in my ear. "What is it? What's out there?" She was trembling all over.

"Chickens," I said, and at that moment three scrawny, brown birds fluttered up to the front window and pecked – *tap, tap, tappitty tap* – on the glass. Ally shrieked and scrambled under the table.

Tap! Tap! Tappitty tap! There were chickens at the back window too. We could see their eyes glinting as their heads squirmed to and fro peck, peck pecking, peck, peck pecking.

The girls went on screaming, and under the table Ally covered her ears with her hands. *Tap! Tap! Tappitty tap!* The sharp little hammer blows filled my mind, and I couldn't think straight . . .

"They'll break the glass!" Laura screeched. "Then they'll get us!"

Something clicked in my brain. An idea. I ran to the back window and pulled the torn and dusty curtain across it. Then I did the same at the front. There was a sudden deathly silence from outside. Inside, all I could hear was my breathing and the girls' whimpering.

"What'll we do?" Susie moaned. "They're all round the house!"

Tiff gave me a furious glare. "It's all your fault, Charlie. If you hadn't shut Mum and Dad in the shed they'd be here and they'd know what to do!"

"Mum! Dad!" sobbed Molly, "I want Mum and Dad!"

"Me too!" Laura wailed.

"And me . . ." Tiff was hanging on to Susie's arm.

"And me . . ." Susie joined in the chorus.

I looked at my sisters. Ally crouched terrified under the table, and the other four heaped together in the middle of the room, wailing for Mum and Dad.

It was now or never.

"I know how to get rid of the chickens," I said.

Ally believed me, but the others didn't. They didn't believe me for ages.

Or wouldn't.

"Tell them, Molly." I kept on and on at her. "Tell them what happened when you got up this morning! Tell them about the four chickens turning back into one!"

 82

Molly whimpered and wriggled but she wouldn't say a word. In the end I lost my temper.

"OK," I shouted. "I'll open up the curtains and you can get rid of them yourselves!" I strode towards the front window.

That did it.

Molly moved away from Laura's side and came to stand by me.

"It's true," she whispered. "I did see it. Four of the birds went kind of *whoompf*! and three of them disappeared . . ."

Laura made a disbelieving snort, but Tiff came to join Molly. Sometimes – if not very often – I'm really glad those two are twins.

"If Moll says it's true, then I believe it as well," she said.

Susie was looking puzzled. "You mean that if we're nice to each other then the chickens go away?"

"Sort of," I said.

Susie shrugged. "Let's try it and see if it

works." She gave Laura a hug, although Laura was stiff as a poker in her arms. "There! Now go and see if they've gone."

I shook my head. "It's no good like that. You have to really believe in what you're doing. You have to mean what you say . . . or do."

"What if we tidy the place up?" Tiff was looking less green now. "What if we make it as nice as we can?" She looked a little shame-faced. "I mean, we haven't exactly been helpful. Mum did look tired last night."

"That would be good," I said.

A voice floated out from under the table. "Do you know what? I know what you've been! You've all been *mean*!" Ally sniffed loudly. "I was in the bed next to Mum last night and she cried for ages and ages. She had her head in her pillow, but I could still hear her."

There was a long and thoughtful silence.

"Mum did say you'd be OK today," I offered. "She said she knew you wouldn't really let Dad down."

 84

The silence went on . . . and then Laura said, "I'll scrub the pans!"

It wasn't brilliant by the time we'd finished, but it was a whole WHOLE lot better. Laura said no one was to open the curtains until the house was as clean as it could be but I could see what was going on outside from the bedrooms where Ally and I were madly shaking blankets and sweeping up dust.

When we began there must have been hundreds of chickens out there. And I mean hundreds.

By the time we'd finished there were eight.

Eight?

That's right.

There were four scrawny brown chickens with long yellow legs scratching about in the weeds. The speckly one and the black-and-white one were clucking about near the shed. And there was a pretty black hen with fluffy tail feathers sitting on top of the shed preening herself and last of all there was a magnificent bird who was nearly twice the size of all the others. That one was strutting about the garden with a kind of "I own this place and don't you forget it" look on its face.

I rushed downstairs.

"It's FINE!" I shouted. "They've all gone! Open the curtains, Moll!"

Molly was cooking a pot of spaghetti sauce. She had a quick peep round the edge of the

battered velvet, and then smiled a huge smile.

"Tan tarra!!!!!!" she shouted, and flung back the curtain.

Tiff did the same at the other window.

"HURRAH!" We yelled and cheered and yelled again as we saw the very, very ordinary chickens in our muddy, weedy garden.

"Phew!" Laura said, and she collapsed on a chair.

"How's the spaghetti?" asked Ally. "I'm starving!"

"Me too," said Susie.

"You'd better let Mum and Dad out," Tiff told me. "After all, it was you who shut them in!"

A faint flutter bubbled up in my chest as I went across to the shed. Mum and Dad had been in there for *hours*. They'd be *furious* . . .

I unbolted the door, and opened it . . .

Mum and Dad were stretched out in the

armchairs, dead to the world.

"OI!" I called. "Don't you want something to eat?"

They yawned, and stretched.

"Hi, Charlie," Mum said, and she smiled. "Ooooh – I do feel better! Is there really something to eat?"

"Spaghetti Bolognese," I said. "And there's a surprise for you, too."

Mum helped Dad stagger back to the cottage. Of course he had to stop to look at the chickens.

"There are two new ones," I said.

"I can see," Dad said. "Fine fellow, that rooster. Let's hope he stays!"

Mum nodded. "I like the little black hen," she said. "She looks old enough to lay – we might have an egg or two if she decides she likes it here."

Dad didn't answer. He was watching the rooster organizing the chickens away from the weeds and into the run.

"Hmm," he said. "Bit of an old bossy boots, isn't he?"

"Yes," said Mum.

Dad rubbed his chin. "I was thinking," he said, "that is, I was before I went to sleep. Maybe I was a bit . . ." His voice trailed away.

"Like the rooster?" Mum suggested gently.

Dad rubbed his chin again. "A bit like the rooster," he agreed. "Maybe I should have talked to all of my chickens before I took this cottage."

Mum took his arm. "That's my Pete," she said.

"We could talk about it over lunch," Dad said. "That is – is it lunch we're going to have, Charlie?"

"I'm not sure," I said. "Lunch or tea. Or both."

"Sounds good to me," Mum said.

Dad was peering at the black-and-white chicken. "Do you know what, Marion?" he said. "I think this one's a rooster too!"

Mum nodded. "I think you're right."

"There!" said Dad, and he almost straightened up completely. "There! I DO know about chickens!"

Mum laughed, and squeezed his arm as the two of them walked together into Cluck Cottage to eat spaghetti.

Me?

I gave my rooster a thumbs up, and ran after them . . .